Cosmo B. Henderson

What ARE You
Doing

W   in
Illustrated by Ned Woodman

Published by Pearson Education Limited, Edinburgh Gate, Harlow, Essex, CM20 2JE
Registered company number: 872828

www.pearsonschools.co.uk

Text © Joanna Nadin 2011

Designed by Bigtop
Original illustrations © Pearson Education 2011
Illustrated by Ned Woodman

The right of Joanna Nadin to be identified as author of this work has been asserted by her in
accordance with the Copyright, Designs and Patents Act 1988.

First published 2011

17

10 9 8 7

British Library Cataloguing in Publication Data
A catalogue record for this book is available from the British Library

ISBN 978 1 408 27409 5

Copyright notice

Printed and bound in China by Golden Cup

Acknowledgements
We would like to thank the children and teachers of Bangor Central Integrated Primary School,
NI; Bishop Henderson C of E Primary School, Somerset; Brookside Community Primary
School, Somerset; Cheddington Combined School, Buckinghamshire; Cofton Primary School,
Birmingham; Dair House Independent School, Buckinghamshire; Deal Parochial School, Kent;
Newbold Riverside Primary School, Rugby and Windmill Primary School, Oxford for their
invaluable help in the development and trialling of the Bug Club resources.

The author and publisher would like to thank the following individuals and organisations for
permission to reproduce photographs:

Cover background © Photocell/Shutterstock; cover notebook image © Klikk/iStockphoto;
inside front cover photo © Joanna Nadin/Mark Pringle

Every effort has been made to contact copyright holders of material reproduced in this book.
Any omissions will be rectified in subsequent printings if notice is given to the publishers.

FRIDAY 3RD DECEMBER

WHAT I WANT FOR CHRISTMAS
by Cosmo B. Henderson

1. A new name. I mean, what's wrong with Tom or Jack? It wouldn't matter so much if the "B" stood for Billy or Bob or Ben. But no, my middle name is "Brilliant" and I am NOT EVEN JOKING.

2. My little sister Dido to start wearing uniform instead of random costumes because there is NOTHING COOL about being followed around by an egg box-headed alligator every break.

3. Kirk Perry to have a brain transplant. Because the one he has at the moment keeps telling him to tie me to the drainpipe outside the school office. Which *FUNNILY ENOUGH* I do not enjoy.

4. Misty Meadows to be able to keep secrets. Because it's bad enough that my best friend is a GIRL and FREAKISHLY tall, but she cannot help telling EVERYONE EVERYTHING.

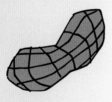

Like when I told her I once got a peanut stuck up my nose and had to go to hospital to get it out, and by last break the whole school was calling me "peanut brain".

5. Lucinda Atkins to notice me in a GOOD way. Because at the moment she mostly says stuff like, "Cosmo B. Henderson, you are such an UTTER WEIRDO." And it wouldn't matter so much if I didn't notice good stuff about her. But the thing is, I sort of do. Misty says it is chemistry and there is nothing I can do about it. She read it in a magazine. I think it's just her hair, which is really long and swishy.

Obviously I didn't hand this list in to Miss Singh-Jones. I wrote another one with stuff like "world peace" and "a games console" on it, like everyone else (even though there's no way Mum would ever get me a games console because she says computer games melt your brain).

The annoying thing is, Lucinda Atkins is right. I AM an UTTER WEIRDO. Mum says it's important to stand out in life, but I think it would be better if we ALL faded into the background, so that I could get through Year 6 without being the class FREAK. But I'm pretty sure there is NO chance of that EVER happening.

It's like Misty says: "Cosmo B. Henderson, YOUR LIFE SUCKS."

SATURDAY 4TH DECEMBER

I have thought of another thing to add to my list:

6. A new dog, because our dog, Paxman, is just EMBARRASSING. For a start, he is a Labradoodle (which sounds made up, and probably should be, but totally ISN'T). On top of that he has dyed ginger hair, because Mum decided to henna him when she did her own hair, and so now he is like this curly orange clown wig on legs.

AND as if that wasn't enough, he
EATS ANYTHING. Seriously.
So far this morning he has eaten an
orange, a gas bill and a fork. Mum
says at least the last one shows some
sense, but she is wrong. I mean, I bet
Kirk Perry's dog, Killer, doesn't eat gas
bills. Only mortal enemies. Like me.

SUNDAY 5TH DECEMBER

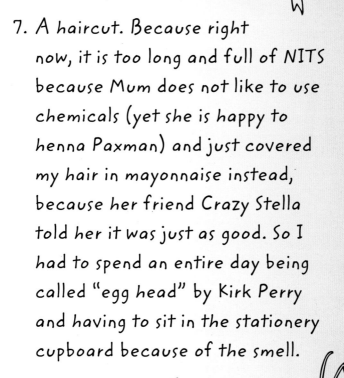

And another thing:

7. A haircut. Because right
   now, it is too long and full of NITS
   because Mum does not like to use
   chemicals (yet she is happy to
   henna Paxman) and just covered
   my hair in mayonnaise instead,
   because her friend Crazy Stella
   told her it was just as good. So I
   had to spend an entire day being
   called "egg head" by Kirk Perry
   and having to sit in the stationery
   cupboard because of the smell.

Plus, FUNNILY ENOUGH, it DID NOT WORK, which is unsurprising given that it was CRAZY Stella's idea (I mean, the clue is in the name), so now my head is like something from a horror film.

Oh, and Mum says she CANNOT cut my hair because she has had a scissor phobia ever since she accidentally snipped a bit off her brother's toe when she was seven. SERIOUSLY. So I will have to wait until she can book me in with Julie from next door who works at Curl Up And Dye.

MONDAY 6TH DECEMBER

Our class is going totally MAD with excitement because Miss Singh-Jones says we are allowed an end of term disco after all, because Mr Grimes, the caretaker, has fixed the pipes that broke when Kirk Perry tried to recreate a tidal wave inside the school hall.

Misty says a disco is an excellent opportunity to try out her chemistry theory with me and Lucinda Atkins because I can ask her to dance. She says that if there is electricity I will know for sure that she is THE ONE, and it is not just the swishiness of her hair that is mesmerising me.

Only I said that it is all very well testing out scientific theories but I am not sure that Lucinda Atkins will agree: (a) if I am wearing anything out of my wardrobe because, apart from my skinny jeans, most of it is multicoloured from the day Misty and I decided to tie-dye everything, and anyway, my skinny jeans have gone mysteriously missing, possibly inside Paxman. And: (b) unless I get a haircut, but Julie from next door says she will not do it if I am infested again. So Mum says it will have to be Deedee Dent at Loose Ends because she is short-sighted and will not see the nits. Only I pointed out that this meant she also would not see my hair to cut it properly, so I am in a total NO WIN situation.

TUESDAY 7TH DECEMBER

It was Misty's idea —
the haircut I mean.

We were in Science and supposed to
be cutting up bits of cardboard to make
into a model of an oil rig, only Miss
Singh-Jones had to take Kirk Perry to see
Mr Phelps, our head teacher, because
he threatened to cut Lyndon Jones' leg
off. And Misty said she knew how to do
haircuts because she'd read about it in a
magazine, and then she just snipped off
a bit at the back and said, "See?"

Then I had this
MASSIVE gap at the
back, so I had to let her
do the rest otherwise I
would have looked WEIRD.

Only now I think I might look even MORE weird because there is only one centimetre left and in some places NO HAIR AT ALL. I mean, at least Kirk Perry's is even, except where he has the arrow shaved into it.

Miss Singh-Jones was not happy at all and sent both of us to Mr Phelps, who was also not happy, but that is probably because he was worried that my mum would blame him and threaten to have a sit-in at school until he couldn't take any more, which is EXACTLY what she did when Dido got sent home by our last head teacher, Mr Crab, for wearing a balaclava. Mum said she was being a postbox, but Mr Crab said it contravened rules on identity and in the end Mum had a sit-in and now Mr Crab has retired early and lives in Spain. Luckily Mum said she was totally on our side because it is our HUMAN RIGHT to cut our own hair whenever we want, even in Science.

Anyway, like I told Mum, at least the nits have gone. Although I am not sure Lucinda Atkins agrees. She said, "Cosmo B. Henderson, you look like a criminal."

WEDNESDAY 8TH DECEMBER

Sometimes I wish Mr Crab was still our head teacher because Mr Phelps is full of BAD ideas. Like now he has decided to have a Mum/Dad/Carer TALENT competition right before the end of term disco to raise money for rescued battery chickens. Lucinda Atkins is totally excited about it because her stepdad is a famous actor in a soap opera (he is a doctor who is secretly in love with his top nurse, only she is an undercover policewoman investigating him for murder), and her mum was once in an advert for shampoo, so she says they are DEFINITELY going to win.

I am NOT EVEN telling Mum about it. If she finds out, my life will be over. Or at least my life for the next nine months until I go to Harold Wilson High, where no one will know about me or about the time Mum made me wear her pants to school because the washing machine was broken.

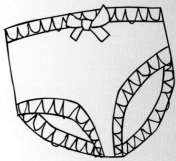

Plus, there is no way Lucinda Atkins is going to test Misty's chemistry theory with me at the school disco if she has just seen Mum doing one of her crazy dances on stage. I mean, what if she thinks that I am going to do weird mime movements too?

Oh, and it is totally a GOOD THING that I have no hair because Dido is scratching again and so is Paxman, and Mum has gone to buy another jar of mayonnaise.

The whole class has gone talent show mad. Lucinda Atkins' mum and stepdad are doing a medley of show tunes, Kirk Perry's dad is going to do a dog show with Killer and even Misty's mum is going to tap dance to 'New York, New York'. I asked Misty if she was going to be embarrassed, but she said only if her mum hits her head on the ceiling, which is totally possible as her mum is also freakishly tall.

Miss Singh-Jones asked what my mum is doing for the show, and I said she isn't allowed to sing or dance because she has purple fever. Which is a total lie, but I really think this is one of those times when lying is OK. Like if your mum says, "Does my bum look big in this?" and you say, "NO," even though it looks HUGE. You are just protecting her. And that is what I was doing. I was protecting me and Mum from a lifetime of SHAME, although she seems to welcome shame. Otherwise why would she bring a mayonnaise-covered, ginger-dyed clown dog to pick me up from school?

And I would have gotten away with it too, except that then Lucinda Atkins put up her hand and said, "Miss Singh-Jones, Cosmo B. Henderson is lying because purple fever is not even REAL and I should know because my stepdad is a DOCTOR." So I said he isn't an ACTUAL doctor, he is an ACTOR doctor. Which even Miss Singh-Jones agreed with. But I was the one who was sent to Mr Phelps because Miss Singh-Jones looked on the internet and realised purple fever is totally made up.

Today I have eaten a sheet of A4 paper. I am NOT EVEN JOKING.

It is because Mr Phelps (who is totally obsessed with EMBARRASSING us all) put a letter in everyone's book bags reminding parents they need to sign up for the talent show by Monday. Which was OK because I was just going to put mine straight into the class recycling box while Miss Singh-Jones was busy telling Kirk Perry off for trying to pencil-sharpen Lyndon Jones' finger, only then I remembered I had to pick up Dido.

As soon as Dido saw me she grabbed my book bag and wouldn't give it back. She said it was her fairy purse (she was wearing wings and a tutu) and couldn't let go or she would DIE, which is ridiculous because why would fairies die if you took their purses?

FAIRY PURSE. SERIOUSLY.

COSMO B. HENDERSON

Anyway, she refused until we got home and she decided to dress up as a Spaniel, and Spaniels don't have purses, so she left it in the bath.

So I got the note out and was totally about to flush it down the loo when Dido came back in and made this speech about how flushing the wrong kind of thing down toilets, like paper or toys, was BAD for the environment and also the plumbing (this is because Rory O'Grady, who is in her class, blocked the infants' toilets up with a plastic turtle last week).

So I told her to be quiet, and then she started shouting and saying I was SUPRESSING her RIGHT TO SPEAK.

Then I panicked because I could hear Mum coming up the stairs, and there is no bin in the bathroom because Dido is using it as a snail house, which is how I ended up eating the talent show letter in a bid to destroy the evidence, which was TOTALLY GROSS and TOTALLY WEIRD.

I would have fed it to Paxman, only he was too busy trying to get some mayonnaise out of his ear. Seriously. He eats ANYTHING. Once he ate the TV remote control and every time he barked the channel changed. That got a bit annoying when I was trying to watch a cartoon and Paxman kept switching it to a programme about bees.

out

SATURDAY 11TH DECEMBER

I am BORED.
This is because
normally on a
Saturday Misty
comes over and we
make Knickerbocker
Glories out of
everything in the
fridge and watch
cartoons. Only this
morning when she
rang I told her I had

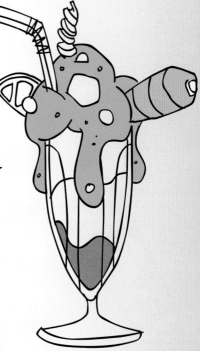

mumps, which is another lie, but I know
if she comes over she won't be able to
RESIST telling Mum about the talent
show, so it is in a GOOD CAUSE.

Although maybe I do have mumps
because I don't feel that well, and I was
a bit late with having my vaccinations

because when I was five Mum decided she didn't believe in vaccinations. She said it was her HUMAN RIGHT to refuse them, and she was never letting anyone else in the family go near a needle ever since Paxman had a flu jab and then ate an egg timer on the same day.

Which is what she told Dr Braithwaite. Only he asked if she'd rather I spend weeks covered in spots with a hacking cough or possibly even DEAD. And Mum had a panic that I was going to die, so the next week she booked me an appointment, only Dr Braithwaite couldn't see me for two months because of the swine flu epidemic.

Anyway, the point is, all I have to do now is keep Misty away from the house until next Friday and everything will be fine and life will be back to normal. Or as normal as it gets when you are called Cosmo, and your sister thinks she's a dog, and your dog thinks it's a waste disposal unit.

SUNDAY 12TH DECEMBER

OK, so on the good side, I don't have mumps. It was just the sheet of paper making me feel strange, but it's out now, which I won't go into. Also, I'm not bored any more. But on the BAD side, MUM KNOWS ABOUT THE SHOW.

This is because Mrs Meadows, i.e. Misty's mum, wanted to go into town to get Misty's Christmas present and needed to do it in PRIVATE (which is pointless as Misty already knows she is getting roller blades, because her mum is as bad as she is when it comes to keeping secrets). Anyway, she rang Mum and asked if she could mind Misty for a bit, and before I could puff my cheeks out to look mumpish, Mum said YES.

So then Misty arrived and she was OK for a bit because I made her stay in my room and play chess (only there

are no chess pieces because Paxman
ate most of them so we have to use jelly
beans and plastic bricks, which is kind
of complicated).
But then Mum
said lunch was
ready, and halfway
through eating the
cheese and asparagus tart, Misty starts
going on about how her mum has got
a gold leotard off Mrs Goldstein next
door and is going to do this bit with a
top hat and a cane. So then Mum asks
why Misty's mum is doing anything with a
gold leotard and a top hat etc. and Misty
just blabs EVERYTHING.

So now Mum is TOTALLY ANNOYED
with me for not telling her before and
also TOTALLY EXCITED about the show
and is RIGHT NOW thinking up her act
with Dido. Which means it will probably

involve dog
outfits or singing
songs about dead
sheep, which is

what Dido has been doing all morning.

Misty says at least she lasted two
hours, which is a new record. But, like I
said, that doesn't make up for the fact
that come Friday I AM
GOING TO DIE. Or possibly
worse, WISH I WAS DEAD.

Misty says I am being
NEGATIVE and I should
concentrate on positive
action, i.e. finding my skinny jeans for
the disco. So we did a forensic search
of the whole house and found £3.57 in
change, a telephone
and a stuffed fox, but
NOT my skinny jeans.

So then we went through my wardrobe and have narrowed it down to three choices:

1. a pair of shorts and an anorak
2. karate kit
3. school uniform.

Misty says it's not about what you wear, which is true. Only I still don't think Lucinda Atkins is going to want to dance with someone in wet weather gear or karate whites.

MONDAY 13TH DECEMBER

Something has compromised the scientific experiment, i.e. Kirk Perry has asked Lucinda Atkins to the disco. SERIOUSLY. Misty says there is NO WAY she will say yes because his whole family are scary - his nan even went to prison! But I pointed out that his nan only went to prison for a day because she didn't pay her council tax and at least the shaving on his head is even.

Oh, and Mum has put her name on the sign-up sheet for the talent show. Lucinda Atkins came up to me right away and demanded to know what talent my Mum had. I said it was a secret (which it is, because Mum is refusing to tell me so that, "it will be a surprise on the night," which is worse if

you ask me) so Lucinda swished her hair
and said, "Well, I don't expect SHE went to
the Fawcett Academy for Dramatic Arts
like my stepdad, or was ever in a shampoo
advert." And then, for some reason, I said,
"That's what you think. Actually she is
pretty amazing, my mum, so you had better
watch out." Then Lucinda Atkins got all
red in the face and swished her hair so
hard it whipped Pippa Ridgeby in the eye,
and then she said, "Cosmo B. Henderson,
you are SUCH a liar."

Then she stormed off and Pippa
Ridgeby had to go to Mr Phelps to sit
down for a bit because she couldn't see.

WHY did I say that? WHY? Because: (a) now Lucinda Atkins will definitely say YES to Kirk Perry and NO to my scientific experiment.

And: (b) I am pretty sure that Mum has NO talent whatsoever. I mean, the last time she did acting, she was pretending to be a horse with Dido and it was totally NOT convincing at all. I mean, since when do horses moo?

MOO

Misty says I need to look on the positive side. But like I said, I've got just four days to AVERT DISASTER and where is the positive in that?

TUESDAY 14TH DECEMBER

Lucinda Atkins has told Kirk Perry
she will NOT go to the disco with him
because: (a) he eats bees
which is cruel (this is
true, I have seen him do
it, only it wasn't to be
cruel, it was to prove he is
immune to pain),

and (b) she likes someone
else. Part of me thought
that maybe, just maybe,
it was me. Only most of me
thought that it was probably
Lyndon Jones because he has a black
belt in karate and a horse. But Misty
says this is definitely positive side
NUMBER ONE. And positive side
NUMBER TWO is that if it was up to
Captain Fabulous (who is this superhero
in a comic book, who she is totally

COSMO
LUCINDA

obsessed with) he wouldn't sit around
feeling totally sorry for himself. He
would come up with a plan of action.
I said, "I bet Captain Fabulous' mum
doesn't try to kill nits with mayonnaise,"
but Misty said I was being NEGATIVE
again and that wouldn't solve anything.
Which she is right about. Annoyingly.

So at lunch, when everyone else was swapping football stickers or pretending to be pop stars, we wrote our ACTION PLAN TO AVERT DISASTER. It looks like this:

Plan A

Create an emergency so that Mum has to deal with that and CAN'T GO TO THE SHOW.

Plan B

Be ill so that Mum has to look after me and CAN'T GO TO THE SHOW.

Plan C

Sabotage the school so that Mr Phelps has to cancel everything and Mum CAN'T GO TO THE SHOW.

Tomorrow we're going to try Plan A — create an emergency. We are going to help Paxman run away. Well, not really run away, but just go missing for a while. Because if he goes missing, then Mum will HAVE to spend the rest of the week looking for him because she says Paxman is "like a son" to her. Even if he does have curly orange hair and ate a stapler and two lumps of coal this morning. Which, I pointed out, I would never do, but Mum said she would love me even if I ate the kitchen sink. Which I guess is actually pretty good, given that I swallowed a sheet of A4 paper four days ago.

WEDNESDAY 15TH DECEMBER

So Plan A didn't QUITE work out.

It started off OK. Misty and I offered to take Paxman for a walk straight after school. Mum was busy making a beaver helmet with Dido so she said, "That's very kind of you, Cosmo B. Henderson," which made me feel kind of bad, but not bad enough not to do it. So we walked all the way into town, and Misty was going to let him off the lead in the hardware

shop, because there are a lot of weird things he likes to eat in there, but I said we should go to the library because it is on three floors and once I got lost for an hour in the history section. So then we thought up pros and cons for each place, only by the time we had decided on the library, we realised Paxman had disappeared anyway. We looked in the hardware shop and in the library, but he was TOTALLY missing. And I know that was the point, except then it didn't seem like such a good idea any more because I felt REALLY sick about Paxman being lost and no one helping him, because he looks so weird and mostly people just laugh.

Then Misty went home because she had a tuba lesson, and I walked round the park for a bit shouting, "Paxman, Paxman." Mr Wrigley from Number 34, who was walking his dog, Muffet, (who is brown and a Yorkshire Terrier, i.e. TOTALLY NORMAL) kept giving me funny looks like he thought I was UP TO NO GOOD. He thinks all children are usually UP TO NO GOOD, although in the case of Kirk Perry he is usually right. So I went home. But UNBELIEVABLY, when I got there, Paxman was ALREADY HOME and was sat on the sofa watching the news.

NORMAL

I asked Mum what he was doing there, and she said, "He likes the weather report for some reason." So I said, "Not ON THE SOFA, I mean AT HOME, because I thought he was lost." And Mum said, "Someone called Mrs Potts accidentally sat on him on the bus after her Senior Swim and brought him home!"

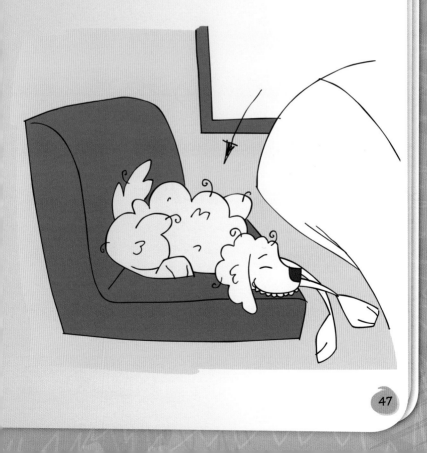

And then she said, "But WHAT was he doing on a bus in the first place, Cosmo B. Henderson? That's what I'd like to know." So I said, "Maybe he felt like having an adventure," and Mum agreed that that was the sort of unique thing Paxman might do. To be honest, I felt relieved because even though he is a ginger clown dog who eats furniture, he is kind of funny.

BUS PASS

Only now I only have TWO DAYS left to avert disaster. Misty says I am being NEGATIVE again, and tomorrow we can do Plan B. Which she's right about.

And she's right about something else as well. Captain Fabulous wouldn't have forgotten to take the address tag off Paxman's collar.

THURSDAY 16TH DECEMBER

We got the idea in History. It was because we were learning all about the Black Death, and Miss Singh-Jones asked us if there were any modern plagues we could think of and Lucinda Atkins, who is always first to answer questions, stuck her hand up and said, "Me, Miss, me," and Miss Singh-Jones looked to see if anyone else wanted to answer but no one did. So she sighed and said, "Yes, Lucinda?" and Lucinda said, "Swine flu, Miss. I know that because my stepdad is a doctor." Miss Singh-Jones said, "That is right, Lucinda." Which meant that she got a gold star (even though her stepdad is NOT an ACTUAL doctor and even though she already has forty-eight. I've only got twenty-three, but at least it's better than Kirk Perry who has eight. He did have nine but one got taken away

when he squeezed
his head between the
railings and got it
stuck and they had to
call the fire brigade
to saw him out).

Anyway, the point is that I am going
to have FAKE swine flu tomorrow
morning so that Mum has to look after
me and can't do the show. Then I am
going to get miraculously better in time
for the disco and Lucinda Atkins will
be so relieved that I am alive, she will
definitely dance with me. Misty says it
is GENIUS, and NOTHING can go wrong.
She had better be right,
otherwise I am going to
wish I had REAL Black
Death, let alone FAKE
swine flu.

FRIDAY 17TH DECEMBER

Something WEIRD has happened. And NOT in the normal sense of WEIRD. But in the weird sense of NORMAL. Which probably won't make sense until you read this:

So to start with, Plan B went TOTALLY to plan.

I thought

at one point

I had overdone it

with the purple spots

on my face

(one of Dido's felt tips),

because I'm not too sure

exactly

what the symptoms

of swine flu are.

But Mum waved her hands over my head and said my aura was definitely damaged and that I had to lie down IMMEDIATELY and drink lavender tea, which is gross and tastes like soap, but BELIEVE ME, it is better than watching Mum embarrass herself (and me) in front of the WHOLE SCHOOL, and especially Lucinda Atkins.

DAMAGED AURA

Then Mum got Julie from next door to take Dido to school, and I could tell Julie wasn't too pleased because Dido was wearing a spacesuit, but she did it anyway because she has to go that way to her job at Curl Up And Dye. So then I got to spend the WHOLE morning on the sofa watching cartoons while Mum rang up Crazy Stella to find out other remedies for swine flu that wouldn't involve REAL medicine. Which for once I was relieved about because I'm pretty sure Dr Braithwaite would not be fooled by the felt tips.

After lunch Mum said she had a brilliant surprise for me, which for one minute I thought actually MIGHT be a games console, because Kirk Perry got one when he had flu, although his mum said it was to shut him up because the whining "did her head in".

But UNSURPRISINGLY the surprise was a lot less brilliant. It was CRAZY STELLA. Mum said she had offered to look after me for the afternoon. And that meant Mum could go and be in the talent show.

I swear I was ALMOST ACTUALLY ILL and I would have begged Mum to change her mind, but she had already whizzed off to school to RUIN MY LIFE and I was left alone with Crazy Stella.

So NOT ONLY was Mum about to SHAME me without me even getting to see it, but I also had to spend several hours with a woman who has a bigger moustache than Mr Crab, and who actually believes in pixies. SERIOUSLY.

I decided I needed to get out of there fast and do Plan C, i.e. sabotage the school, i.e. set off the fire alarms, like Kirk Perry did once in assembly and we all had to stand outside in the rain even though it was OBVIOUS there was no fire because WHERE WAS THE SMOKE?

So I let Stella do a magic chant over me, and then said, "Wow, Stella, I feel amazingly better. In fact, SO much better that I think I could go back to school." And Stella was so pleased that she said, "Brilliant, because I am DYING to see Cherry (i.e. my mum) do her THING." I said, "What is her THING exactly?" But Crazy Stella said,

"Wait and see."

Which made me feel ill all over again. But I didn't have time to worry about that, or the fact that I was about to arrive at school with a woman with a moustache, and a ginger curly clown dog, because I had a show to stop.

When I got to school the hall was PACKED, and I could see the fire alarm behind Miss Singh-Jones, but between me and her were about a hundred people including Kirk Perry and Lucinda Atkins. So I started pushing through them all, and I didn't stop.

Not when Lucinda screamed and said,

"Oh my gosh, it's Cosmo B. Henderson, and he's contagious!"

Not when Kirk Perry tripped me up so that I ended up in Pippa Ridgeby's lap. Not when Miss Singh-Jones said,

"That is four gold stars I am knocking off your tally, young man."

I didn't stop until my finger was touching the fire alarm bell.

But that's when the WEIRD thing happened, because then the whole room went quiet and I heard Mum's voice. And AMAZINGLY it wasn't shouting, "Cosmo B. Henderson, WHAT do you think you are doing?" It was singing. And it was BEAUTIFUL.

I am NOT EVEN JOKING. Mum CAN SING! And not the usual humming she does in the kitchen when she is making tea. This was proper opera stuff, with warbling bits and everything. In fact, she can sing so well that she made Miss Singh-Jones cry.

Plus she totally beat Mr and Mrs Atkins, whose show medley fell apart when Paxman tried to join in, AND Kirk Perry's dad and Killer, who got disqualified for trying to bribe the judges, and EVEN Misty's mum, who didn't hit her head, but did accidentally poke Mr Phelps in the ear with her cane.

But Misty doesn't mind, because, as she says, "Cosmo B. Henderson, your life ISN'T so sucky any more."

And you know what, I think she's right. Even though Paxman ate a microphone and Lyndon Jones' trainers.

Even though Crazy Stella had to be taken to Mr Phelps' office for trying to summon up goblins from under the infants' climbing frame. And EVEN THOUGH it wasn't until I was up on stage that I realised I was STILL WEARING MY PYJAMAS. Which I figured was so NOT the kind of outfit that would make Lucinda Atkins want to do the scientific experiment.

Only the thing is – she DID. She actually DANCED with me, once I'd shown her that my spots were felt tip and that I wasn't contagious. And even though it was only one dance, and even though straight after she went off with Lyndon Jones because he promised she could ride his horse tomorrow, and even though I am pretty sure there were no actual sparks or anything, which is what Misty said there would be, I think maybe she doesn't hate me. She might even like me. Just a little bit.

So I think I might want world peace for Christmas after all.